SLITHER McCREEP
AND HIS
BROTHER, JOE

WRITTEN BY
TONY JOHNSTON

ILLUSTRATED BY
VICTORIA CHESS

SLITHER McCREEP
AND HIS
BROTHER, JOE

VOYAGER BOOKS

HARCOURT BRACE & COMPANY

SAN DIEGO   NEW YORK   LONDON

First Voyager Books edition 1996
Voyager Books is a registered trademark of Harcourt Brace & Company.

Library of Congress Cataloging-in-Publication Data
Johnston, Tony.
Slither McCreep and his brother, Joe / written by Tony Johnston;
illustrated by Victoria Chess — 1st ed.
p.   cm.
Summary: Young snake Slither McCreep, angry because
his brother, Joe, will not share his toys, reacts
by breaking them and then feels remorse.
ISBN 0-15-276100-4
ISBN 0-15-201387-3 (pbk.)
[1. Snakes — Fiction.   2. Sharing — Fiction.   3. Brothers — Fiction.]
I. Chess, Victoria, ill.   II. Title.
PZ7.J6478Sl   1992
[E] — dc20   90-36792

A C E F D B

Printed in Singapore

For Betty Takeuchi
and her Speckled Band
at the San Marino Toy and Book Shoppe
— T. J.

For Dick Gackenbach and Cog Godwin
with love
— V.C.

Slither McCreep and his brother, Joe, were snakes.
They were of the species *Strangulanus gorgeanus* — that
is, the squeezing kind.

Slither and Joe lived with their mother, who was a
gorgeous squeezer, too. They were happy, except when
Slither and Joe fought.

One day Slither said, "Mom, Joe put a sign on his door. It says NO SLITHERS ALOUD." (Even though it was spelled wrong, it made him furious.)

"Ignore it," said Mother.

Slither did not ignore it. He thought about it all the time.

Later on he said, "Joe won't share his beach ball."

"I need it," said Joe.

"What for?" asked Slither.

"To sit on," said Joe.

"See what I mean, Mom?"

"Ignore it," said Mother.

Slither did not ignore it. He thought about it all the time.

Soon he complained to Mother again. "Joe won't let me use his rat robots."

"I need them," said Joe.

"What for?" asked Slither.

"To do my homework."

"Who does homework with rat robots roaring all over his desk?" wailed Slither.

"I do," said Joe.

Later still, Slither shouted, "Joe won't let me wear his purple sweater!"

"*I'm* wearing it."

Slither gave him a glassy stare.

"On your head?" he said.

"I'm playing sultan."

"The Sultan of Stingies," said Slither.

"If you feel so crabby," said Mother, "go squeeze something. You'll feel much better."

Joe went to watch TV. He took some things he didn't want Slither to use. He wrapped himself around them — *tight*. He watched his favorite rock group, Bal Boa and the Vindow Vipers.

They wore purple capes and rose-colored sunglasses.
They hissed "For Heaven Snakes," "In Cold Blood," and
"Scales, Part II." Joe loved it.

"Wow!" he said. "They're really neat. *Wow!*"

Meanwhile, Mother had given Slither an idea.

"You bet I'll squeeze something," he said to himself, sneaking into Joe's room.

He squeezed Joe's beach ball — POP!

He squeezed Joe's eggshell collection — CRACK!

Then he squeezed Joe's rat robots. He squeezed them
into a big wad — CRUNCH!

Mother was right. He felt better.

For good measure he swallowed Joe's Fun Shape Set —
GULP!

Slither looked in the mirror. He adored being so many
shapes at once.

When the Bal Boa show was over, Joe went to his room. It was full of strange blobs.

Slither was coiled on the floor, smiling.

"Hey!" cried Joe. "Where's my beach ball?"

"I squeezed it," said Slither.

"Where's my eggshell collection?"

"Squeezed."

"My rat robots?"

"*Sssssqueezed,*" said Slither.

"And my Fun Shape Set?" Joe almost screamed.

"I swallowed it. Don't I look great?"

"Hey, Mom!" Joe yelled. "Slither squeezed up all my stuff. And he ate my shape set!"

"Don't have a hissy-fit over it," Slither said.

When Mother saw the damage, she said, "Go to your room, or I'll turn you into a shape that is not much fun."

Slither went to his room. He banged the door — WHANG-O!

Inside, it was quiet. Very quiet.

Slither thought about his rampage.

I should feel good about wrecking Joe's stuff, he thought. *But I feel bad. And Joe feels worse. What should I do now?*

Suddenly he had an idea. It made him happy again. It made him so happy he hissed a little song.

Outside, Joe and Mother heard it.

"Hiss-hiss-a-hiss. Ssst-ssst-a-ssst."

Then they heard a loud KER-POP!

"He squeezed something *else!*" howled Joe.

"There's nothing else to squeeze," Mother
reminded him.

Still, they hurried in to see what had happened.

Slither was coiled on the floor, smiling. Something was broken all around him. Something was smashed to smithereens.

"Now what have you wrecked, you wrecker?" Joe screeched.

"My piggy bank," Slither said. "I'm sorry I broke everything. I'm going to buy you new stuff."

Joe was speechless. His tongue just went in and out, out and in. Again and again.

Mother was not speechless. "What a nice idea," she said. And she gave Slither a little squeeze.

At last Joe said, "I'm sorry, too. I wouldn't share anything."

Slither said, "Well, what do you want to buy?"

Joe's eyes glittered with excitement. He listed the things he wanted.

"Rose-colored sunglasses," he said. "And a purple cape. And a new beach ball."

"Hey, great," said Slither. "Can I use it?"

"I will need it," said Joe.

"What for?"

"To sit on."

Slither looked at Joe.

"Are you joking?" Slither asked.

"Yes," said Joe.

Then they both had a hissy-fit — of giggles.

The illustrations in this book were done in Winsor & Newton liquid
watercolors, Schmeincke regular watercolors, Prisma pencils,
and Rotring technical inks and pens on Langton watercolor paper
by Daler & Rowney.
The display type was set in Goudy Sans Medium Italic
by Thompson Type, San Diego, California.
The text type was set in Goudy Sans Book
by Thompson Type, San Diego, California.
Color separations were made by Bright Arts, Ltd., Singapore.
Printed and bound by Tien Wah Press, Singapore
This book was printed with soya-based inks on Leykam recycled paper,
which contains more than 20 percent postconsumer waste
and has a total recycled content of at least 50 percent.
Production supervision by Warren Wallerstein and Pascha Gerlinger
Designed by Trina Stahl